CONTENTS

MEET
EMMA

EMMA
Every Day

Bolton
Council

S

Please return/ renew this item
by the last date shown. JF
Books can also be renewed at
www.bolton.gov.uk/libraries

Raintree is an imprint of Capstone Global Library Limited, a company incorporated in England and Wales having its registered office at 264 Banbury Road, Oxford, OX2 7DY – Registered company number: 6695582

www.raintree.co.uk
myorders@raintree.co.uk

ISBN: 978 1 3982 0576 5

Designed by Tracy McCabe
Printed and bound in India
Originated by Capstone Global Library Ltd

Image Credits:
Design Elements: Shutterstock: achii, Mari C, Mika Besfamilnaya
Sign language illustrations by Pixelfox

British Library Cataloguing in Publication Data:
A full catalogue record for this book is available from the British Library.

EMMA CARTER
Age: 8

SIBLING
One brother, Jaden
(12 years old)

PARENTS
David and Lucy

BEST FRIEND
Izzie Jackson

PET
a goldfish named Ruby

favourite colour: teal
favourite food: tacos
favourite school subject: writing
favourite sport: swimming
hobbies: reading, writing, cycling, swimming

FINGERSPELLING
ALPHABET

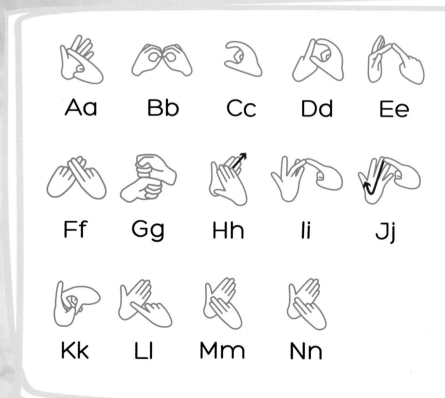

Aa   Bb   Cc   Dd   Ee

Ff   Gg   Hh   Ii   Jj

Kk   Ll   Mm   Nn

Emma is Deaf. She uses British Sign Language (BSL) to communicate with her family. She also uses a Cochlear Implant (CI) to help her hear.

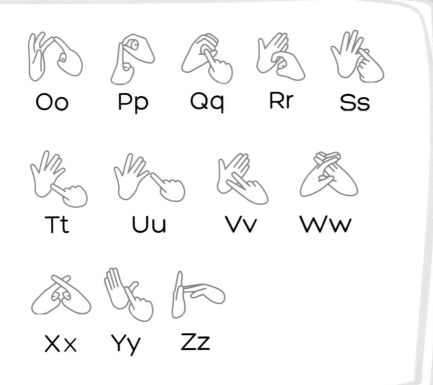

Oo Pp Qq Rr Ss

Tt Uu Vv Ww

Xx Yy Zz

Chapter 1
Apple day

Emma was so excited! Today her dad was taking her to the apple orchard.

Emma's best friend, Izzie, was coming too.

"Are you girls ready?" Emma's dad signed.

"I am," Izzie signed.

Emma put on her Cochlear Implant (CI). Then she grabbed her wellies and coat.

"Me too! Let's go!" Emma said.

As soon as they got to the orchard, it started raining. Farmer Bell drove up in a tractor pulling a trailer filled with hay.

"I'm glad I wore my wellies," Izzie signed.

"Same here!" Emma signed back.

"Are you girls ready?" Farmer Bell signed.

"You know BSL?" Emma signed.

"I do. My daughter is deaf. She works here too," he signed.

Emma and Izzie climbed onto the trailer. An empty basket sat between them. They had to wait while Emma's dad got his basket.

Muddy puddles covered the road.

The trailer bumped along.

"Dad, can we help you make apple treats when we get home?" Emma asked.

"Of course! What kind do you want to make?" Dad asked.

"Apple tarts," Izzie said.

"And apple pies, apple sauce and toffee apples," Emma said.

With a final jolt, the trailer stopped. Farmer Bell helped everyone off the trailer.

"Have fun!" he signed, smiling.

Chapter 2

Apple attack

"Let's go and pick some

yummy apples," Izzie said.

She grabbed their basket and

started down the path. Emma

followed.

The girls picked apples from the lower branches. They picked as many as they could. Emma's dad picked from the higher branches.

"Choose the crunchiest," he said. "They're better for baking."

Bonk!

"Ouch! What was that?" Emma said, rubbing the top of her head.

"You were attacked by an apple," Izzie said, pointing to one on the ground.

Emma made a face and laughed. Then she grabbed the apple off the ground. She popped it into their basket, which was now full.

Emma and Izzie lugged the
basket back to the road. They
flopped onto a bench to wait for
Farmer Bell. But the bench was wet.
Emma slipped right off.

"What a day!" Emma said, laughing.

"At least we still have our apples," Izzie said.

"And lots of them," Emma's dad said.

Minutes later the tractor pulling the trailer rumbled up and stopped. Farmer Bell was back!

The girls put their basket on the trailer and climbed in.

"Hold on!" Farmer Bell called out to the group.

The tractor jerked forwards. The trailer bounced along behind. It hit a big rut, and the girls' basket tipped right off the trailer!

Splash!

All the apples rolled into a muddy puddle!

Chapter 3

Candy

The trailer slowed down and

stopped. Farmer Bell checked the

fallen apples.

"These are no good now,"

he said. "Sorry, girls."

"It's okay. I've still got my apples," Emma's dad said.

"Don't worry. I'll get Candy when we get back to the shop," Farmer Bell said.

"Candy? Is he going to give us candy? Like sweets?" Emma signed to Izzie.

"I don't know," Izzie signed. "But I do like candy."

Ten minutes later, they pulled up in front of Bell's Apple Shop. Farmer Bell hurried inside.

Emma's dad, Emma and Izzie wandered into the shop. A young woman carrying a big bag of apples met them.

"Hello, I'm Candy Bell," she

signed as she handed the bag to

Emma. "My dad said you lost

your apples."

"Thank you," Emma signed.

She noticed Candy had a CI.

"I use a CI too!" Emma signed.

Candy smiled. "I love my CI,
but I still sign most of the time."

"Me too," Emma signed.

"And Emma taught me
BSL," Izzie signed.

"That's great!" Candy signed.

Then Farmer Bell came over with

Emma's dad. They had a tray of

apple treats.

"Dig in," Farmer Bell said.

It was the perfect end to a crazy,

rainy apple orchard day.

LEARN TO SIGN

Emma uses British Sign Language to help her communicate. Different words have their own signs. There are around 15,000 BSL users in the UK. Babies can start to learn sign language from only 8 weeks old! Maybe you already use BSL, or maybe you already know some signs. Have a go at fingerspelling names and words using the alphabet at the start of this book. Then try these signs out too!

Apple

Thanks/Please

FIND OUT MORE

Visit these websites to find out more about sign language:

Communicating with sign language
www.bbc.co.uk/bitesize/clips/zrxqxnb

How to sign the alphabet in British Sign Language
www.bbc.co.uk/bitesize/articles/z6shnrd

National Deaf Children's Society
www.ndcs.org.uk/

GLOSSARY

Cochlear Implant (also called CI) a device that helps someone who is deaf to hear; it is worn on the head just above the ear

communicate to pass along thoughts, feelings or information

deaf being unable to hear

fingerspell to make letters with your hands to spell out words; often used for names of people and places

lugged carried something with lots of effort

rut a deep, narrow track in the ground made by wheels

sign use hand gestures to communicate

sign language a language in which hand gestures, along with facial expressions and body movements, are used instead of speech

TALK ABOUT IT

1. Emma's favourite season is autumn. Talk about your favourite season.

2. A lot of things went wrong for Emma in the story. Do you think she still had a fun day? Why or why not?

3. Were you surprised by the ending of the story? Why or why not?

WRITE ABOUT IT

1. Make a list of at least five activities you like to do during your favourite season.

2. Emma's best friend is Izzie. Write a paragraph about one of your friends.

3. There were a few clues in the story leading up to the apples falling off the trailer and into the mud. Look back and make a list of at least three of those clues.

ABOUT THE AUTHOR

Deaf-blind since childhood,
C.L. Reid received a Cochlear
Implant (CI) as an adult to
help her hear, and she uses sign
language to communicate. She and
her husband have three sons. Their middle son is
also deaf-blind. Reid earned a master's degree in
writing for children and young adults at Hamline
University in St. Paul, Minnesota, USA. Reid lives in
Minnesota with her husband, two of their sons, and
their cats.

ABOUT THE ILLUSTRATOR

Elena Aiello is an illustrator
and character designer. After
graduating as a marketing
specialist, she decided to study
art direction and CGI. Doing
so, she discovered a passion for
illustration and conceptual art. She works
as a freelancer for various magazines and
publishers. Aiello loves video games and sushi
and lives with her husband and her little pug,
Gordon, in Milan, Italy.